THIS BLOOMSBURY BOOK

BELONGS TO

....

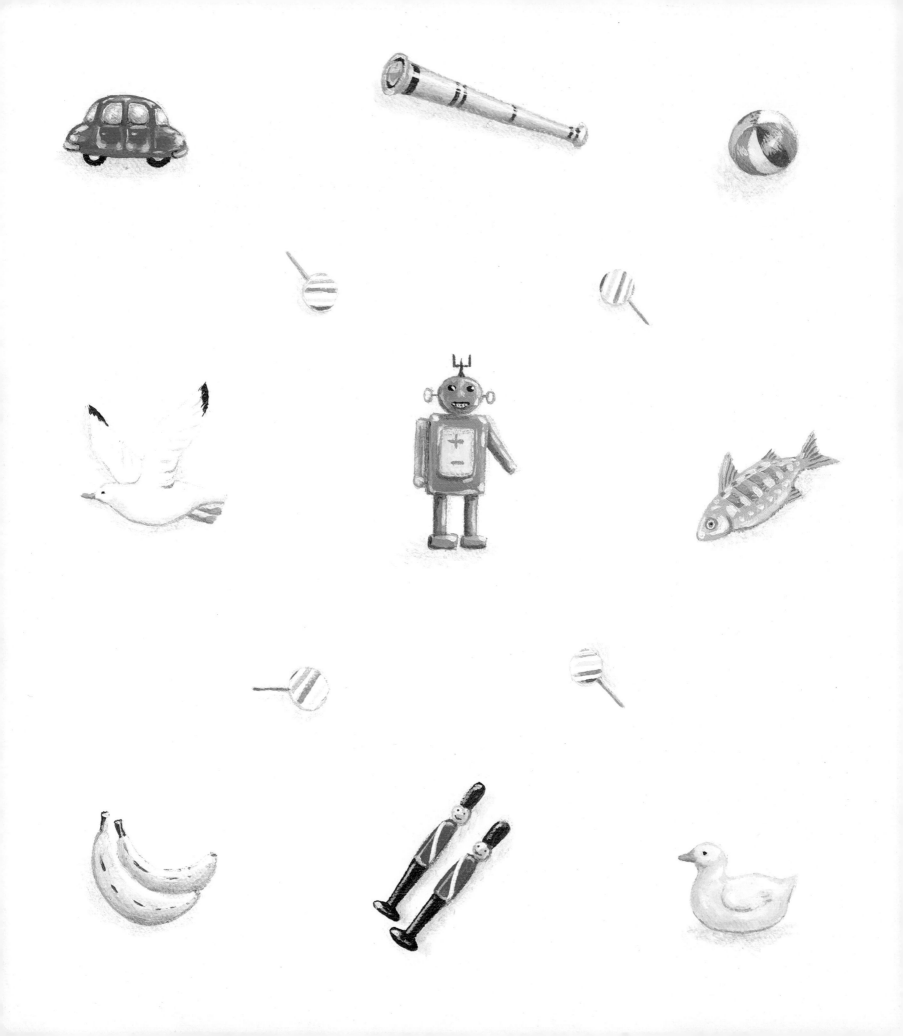

For Max, with love – *AM*

For Bruno, with love – *JJ*

This edition published for Igloo Books Ltd in 2007

First published in Great Britain in 2003 by Bloomsbury Publishing Plc
38 Soho Square, London, W1D 3HB

Text copyright © Angela McAllister 2003
Illustrations copyright © Jenny Jones 2003
The moral rights of the author and illustrator have been asserted

A CIP catalogue record of this book is available from the British Library

ISBN 0 7475 6494 9

Printed and bound in China by South China Printing Co.

3 5 7 9 10 8 6 4 2

All papers used by Bloomsbury Publishing are natural, recyclable products made from wood grown in well-managed forests.
The manufacturing processes conform to the environmental regulations of the country of origin.

Harry's Box

By Angela McAllister

Illustrated by Jenny Jones

Harry helped his mother at the supermarket.
He put all the shopping in the box

and, when they got home, he took
all the shopping out of the box.

So his mother gave Harry the box to play with.
First he put it in the kitchen.

There it was a shop
full of toys, treats and treasures.

But a difficult customer wanted bones and old slippers.

"I can't please everybody," said Harry the Shopkeeper.

Then he put the box in the garden.

There it was a dangerous lion's den
where a roaring lion and a growling bear
waited to frighten somebody.

But only a brave dog passed by
and barked at the wild animals.

"Lions just aren't scary enough,"
sighed Harry the Lion.

So then he put the box in the bathroom.

And there it was a pirate ship
sailing on the stormy seas in search of treasure.

A shipwrecked sailor said there was
something precious buried in the sand.

"I expect it will only be a bone," said Harry the Pirate.

Next he put the box under the table.

There it was a sandy cave
on the seabed where an octopus waved
his arms to catch fish for supper.

But only a dog-fish swam by and
he was far too hairy to eat.

"I hope that it's fish fingers for tea,"
said Harry the Octopus.

Then he put the box in the bedroom.

There it was a castle
on a high hill where a king and
his soldiers were ready for battle.

But when the foe arrived she brought
the king's favourite biscuits.

"Let's make friends,"
said Harry the King.

So then he put the box behind the sofa.

And there it was a warm, snug bed
where Harry and Woolfie dreamt about

dog food

and lions

and pirates

and octopuses

and castles

and all the fun they would have tomorrow...

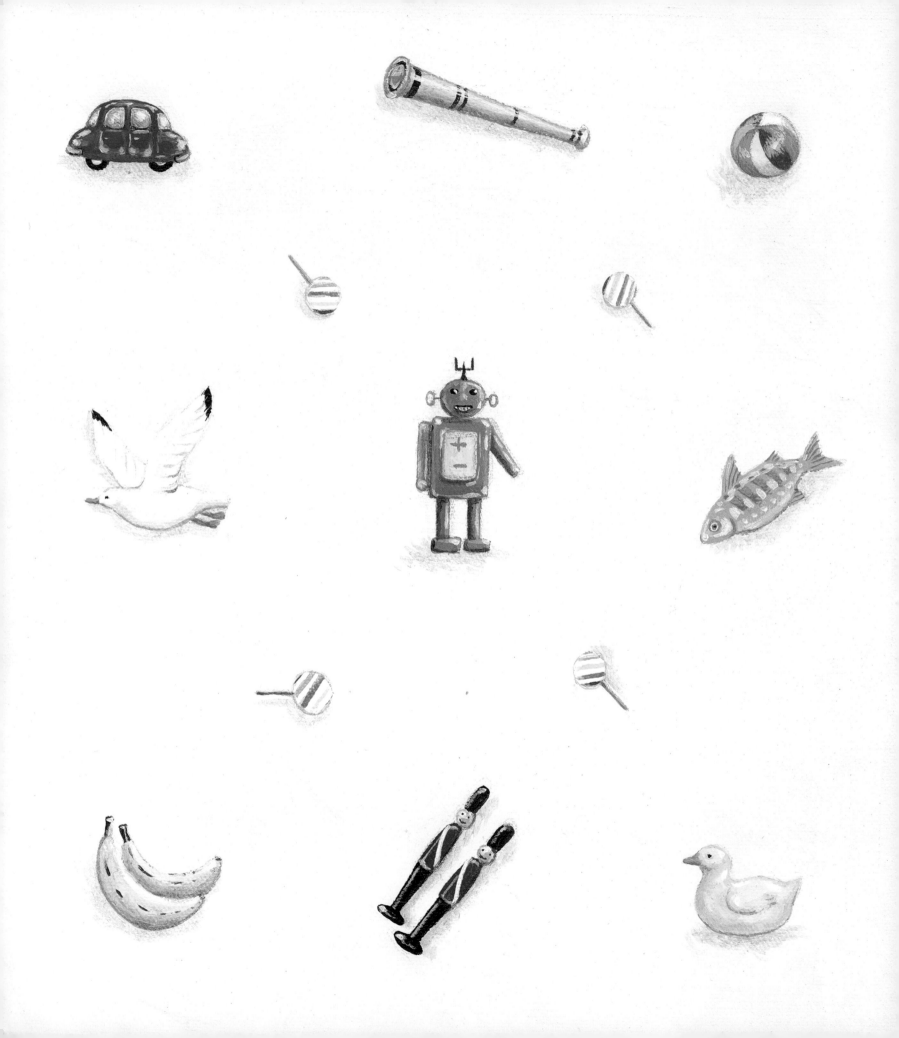

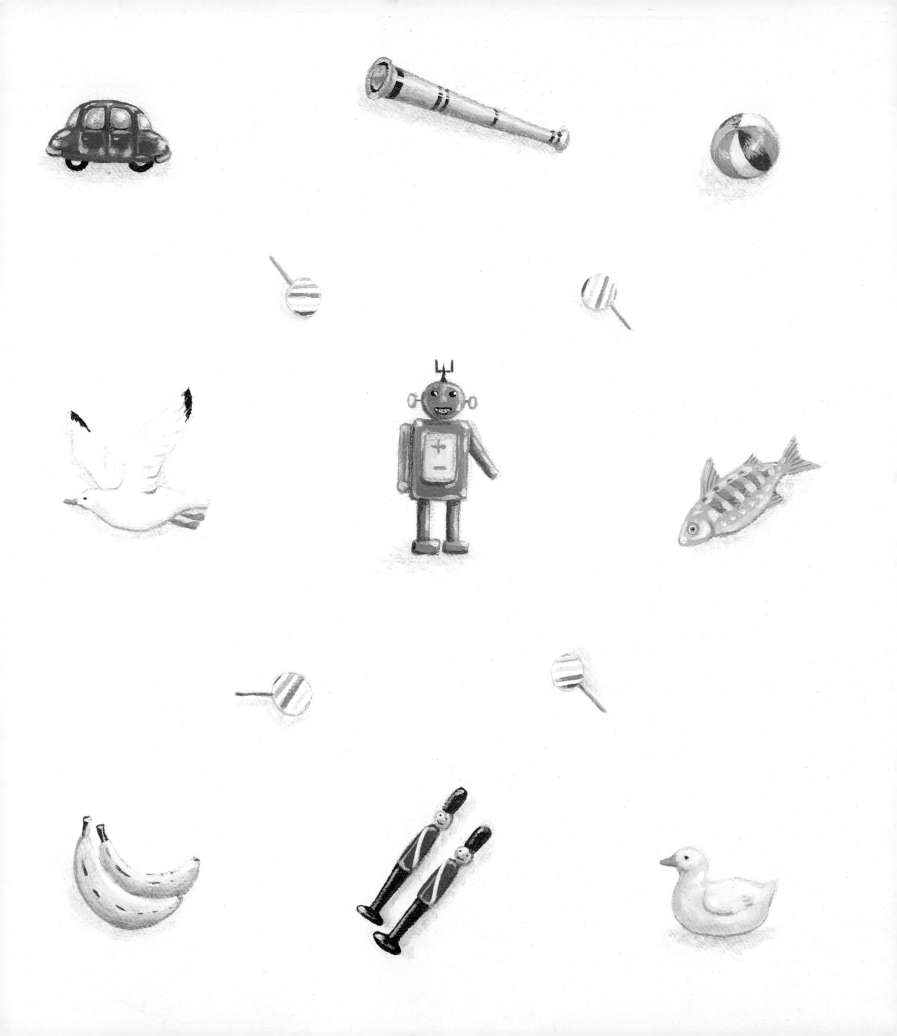

Enjoy more great books from Angela McAllister and Jenny Jones ...

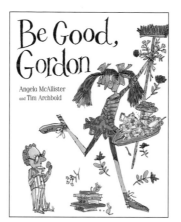

Be Good, Gordon
Angela McAllister &
Tim Archbold

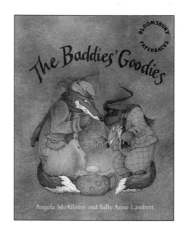

The Baddies' Goodies
Angela McAllister &
Sally Anne Lambert

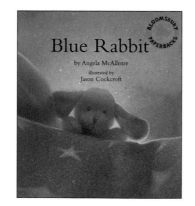

Blue Rabbit
Angela McAllister &
Jason Cockcroft

Sandbear
Shen Roddie & Jenny Jones

All now available in paperback